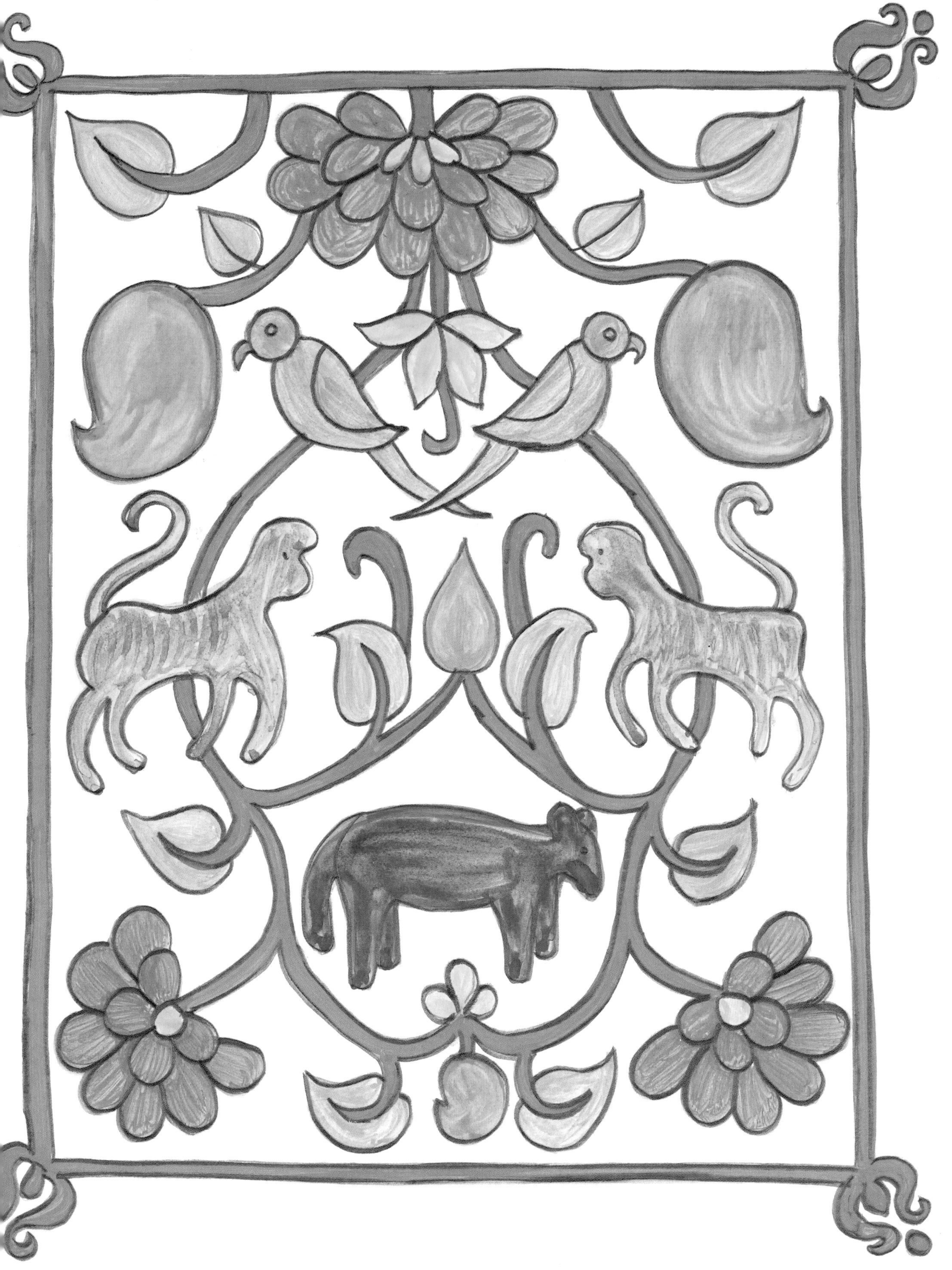

THE
BLUE JACKAL

written and illustrated

by

Rashmi Sharma

Vidya Books
Berkeley, California

Library of Congress Catalog Card Number 92-64170
ISBN 1-878099-50-7 (H)
ISBN 1-878099-51-5 (P)

Published in the United States of America
by
Vidya Books
Post Office Box 7788
Berkeley, CA 94707-0788
USA

To my husband and children for their patience and support, and my friends Karen and Valerie who gave me the courage to go beyond the rejection slips any author gets.

THE
BLUE JACKAL

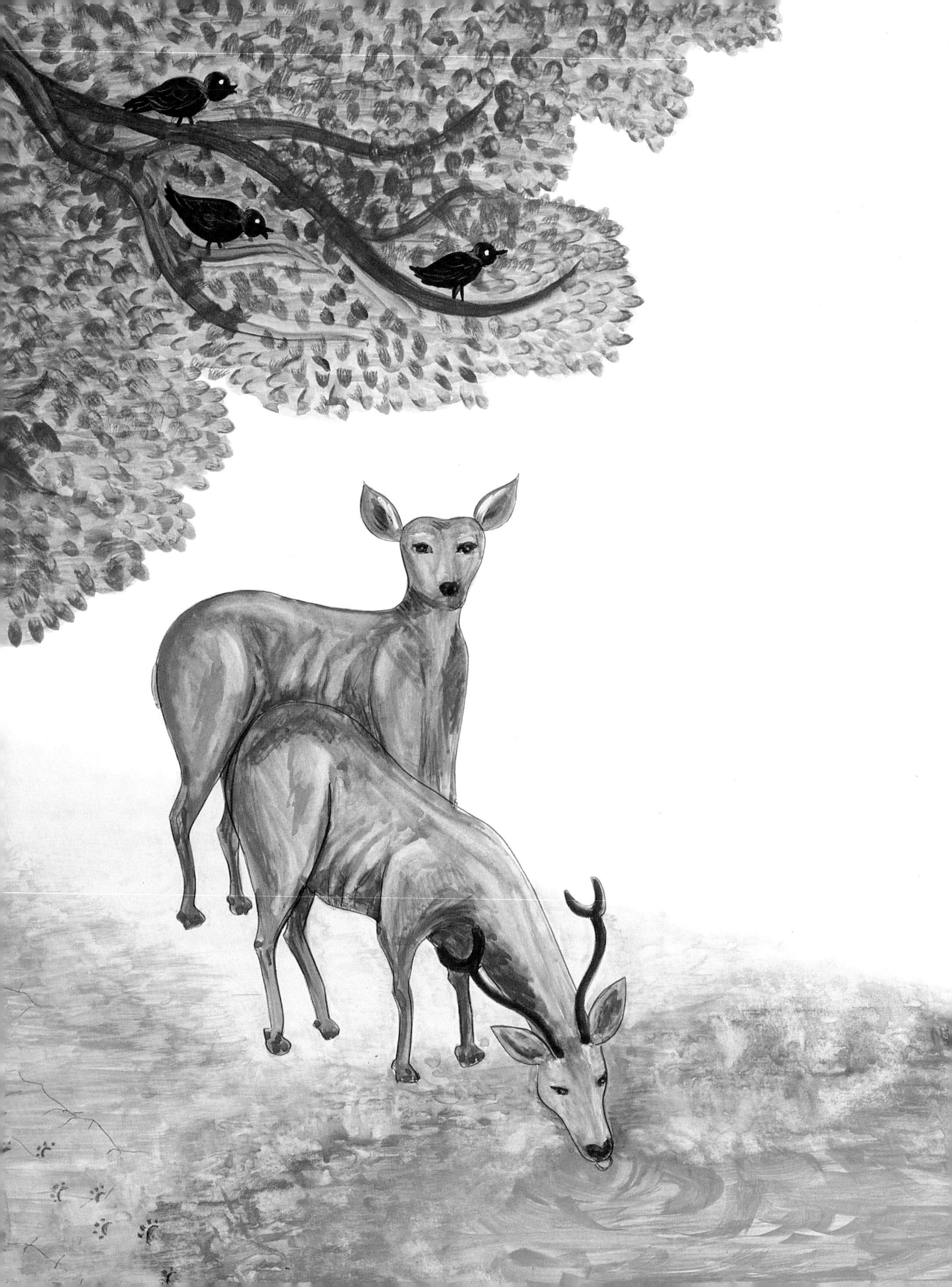

In a jungle far away in India there lived many animals. They were all waiting for the rain to come. The summer had been long and hot, and they were all eager for the monsoon to make the land lush and green once again. The water hole was dry. It was hard to find anything fresh to eat anymore.

This was specially true for a lone jackal. By the end of the summer, he had become so thin that his bones stood out.

One day he decided he would risk going into the outskirts of a small village near the jungle, and maybe there he would be luckier.

The jackal waited until the mid-afternoon heat had lulled man and beast to sleep, and then he crept out in search of food.

Looking carefully both ways, he crossed the clearing behind the first house.

Unfortunately, he found nothing much to eat. He jumped a low wall and landed in the courtyard of the next house. Here, too, the farmer's wife had carefully put away all the food.

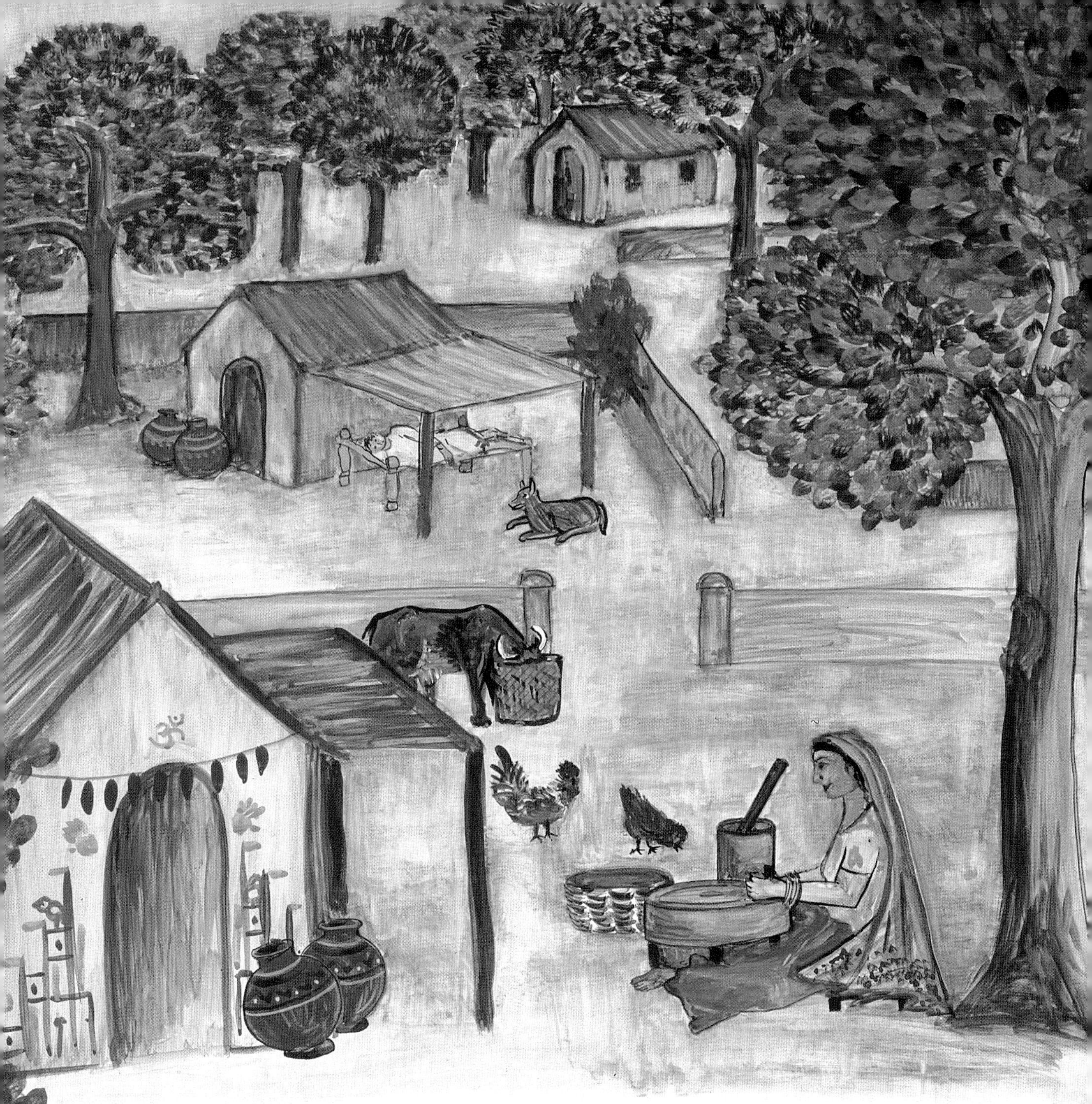

No one had yet come to chase him away. This made the jackal a little bolder. He moved to another backyard.

A sleeping dog, who had been too hot and lazy to try to do anything about a jackal far away, now saw that the jackal was closer. He roused himself to utter a deep growl.

This woke up some of the other dogs. They began to bark and come towards him. The poor jackal was now really scared.

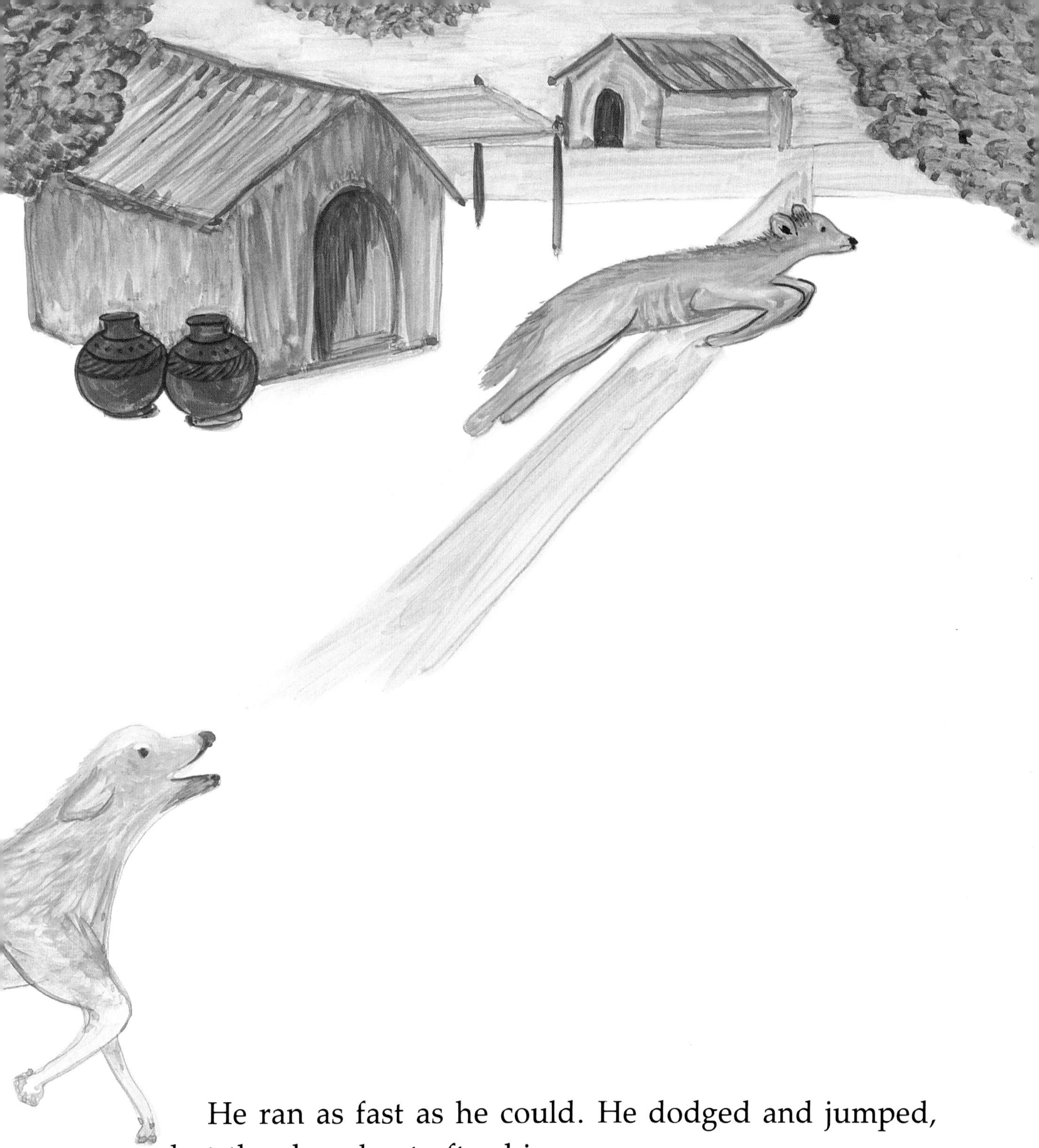

He ran as fast as he could. He dodged and jumped, but the dogs kept after him.

He saw a shed and decided to hide in it. He tried to jump over some tools and tubs but couldn't jump far enough. He landed with a big splash in one of the tubs.

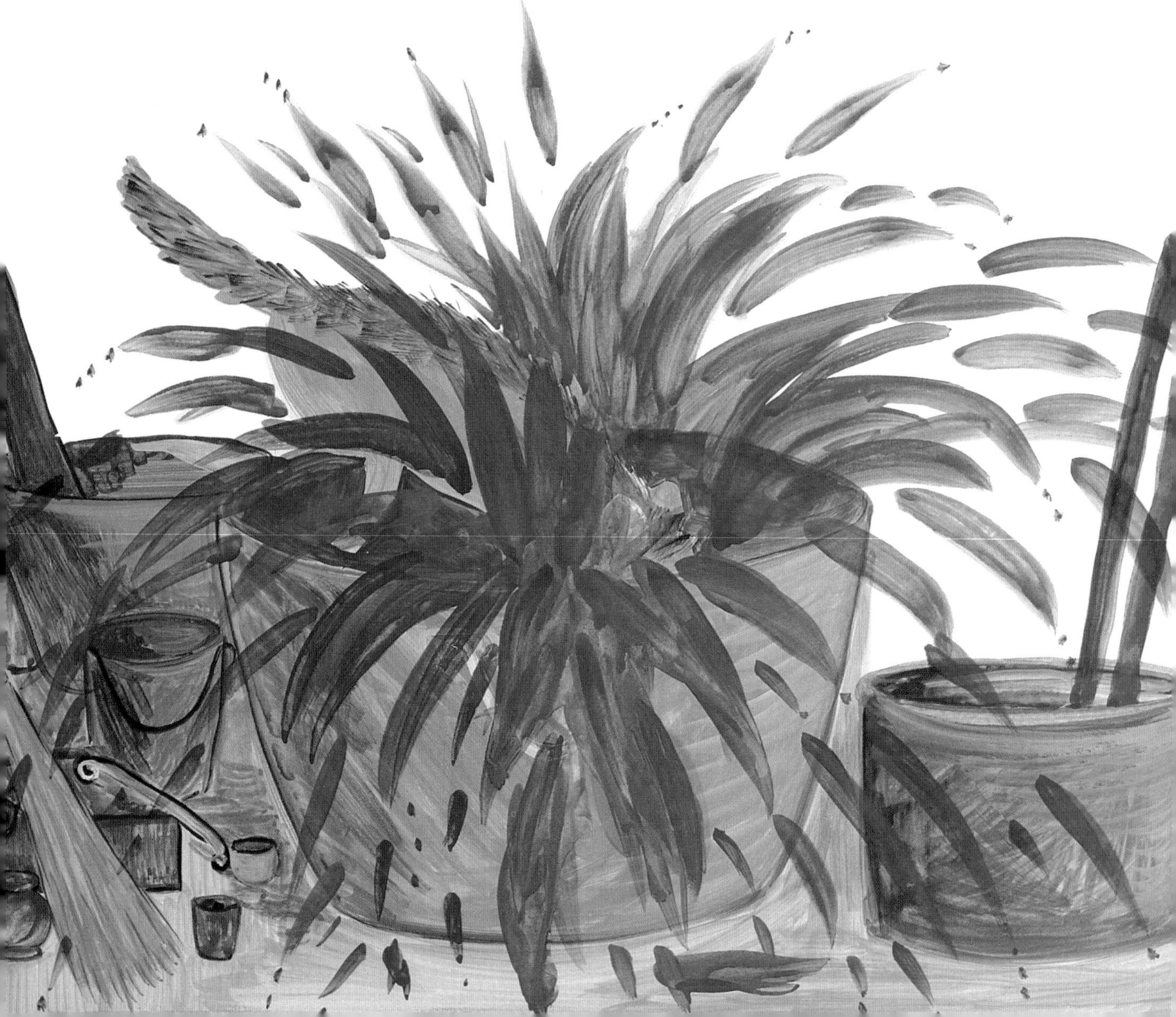

The dogs, who could not get into the vats and tubs, decided to give up the chase and go back to their naps. It was too hot to chase anything anyway!

To the jackal's surprise, the dogs left him alone. Panting hard, he decided to stay put until nightfall and then crawl back to the jungle.

He stayed quietly submerged in the cool blue-colored water in the tub, praying that no one would discover his hiding place before it became dark enough for him to go back to the safety of the forest.

He was lucky. The shed belonged to a man who made his living dyeing clothes into beautiful colors. He has finished dyeing a load of muslin blue that morning, and was on his way to the market in the afternoon to sell his beautiful indigo-colored cloth.

The man's wife and children went with him to enjoy the weekly market. So no one disturbed the jackal in the shed.

Come nighfall, the jackal, who was now blue from the dye in the tub, ventured out.

Carefully and quietly, he made his way to the safety of the jungle. Tired, he fell asleep in the first safe spot he found.

When he woke up, the sun was shining.

He gave a start!

Why was his leg blue?

Good heavens! His whole body seemed to have turned blue!

He tested his limbs – nothing seemed to be broken. He felt tired, but otherwise alright.

Well, never mind the blue color, he thought, hunger pangs givings his thoughts a different direction.

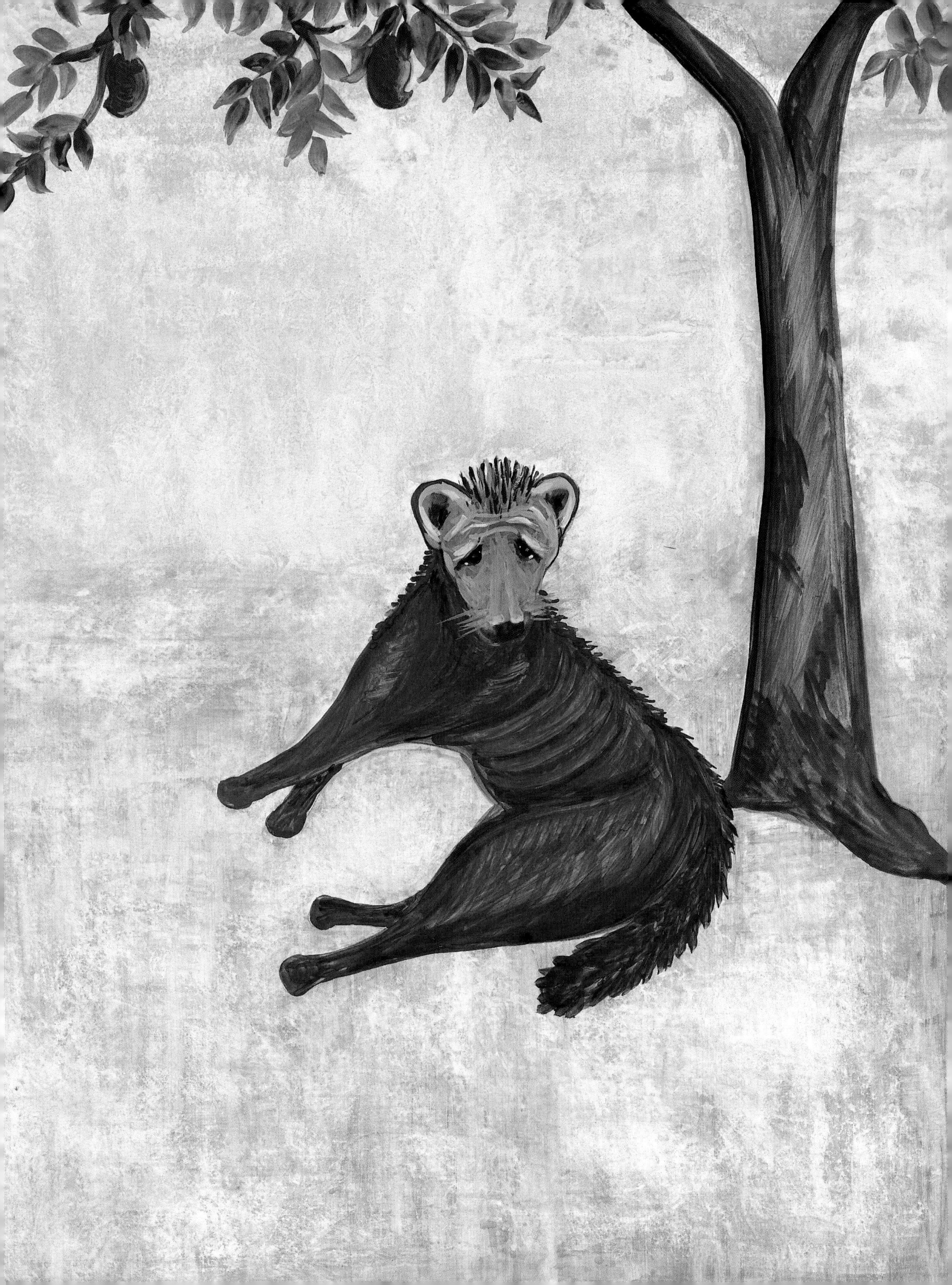

When this hungry blue jackal went looking for food, another surprise awaited him. Many of the animals were scared of him. As soon as they saw him coming, they would scurry away, and hide.

From a safe distance they would study this strange colored creature. He looked like a jackal, but his bright blue color was most unusual. What kind of a creature was he?

The animals had never seen a blue jackal before.

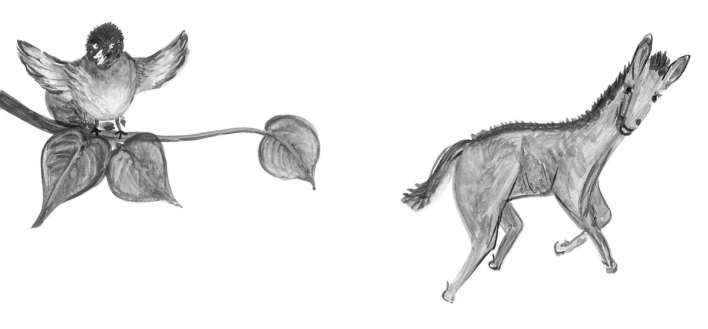

When the animals scurried away, they left behind their food.

For once the jackal ate what he wanted, and the other animals ate *his* leftovers!

The jackal decided that this was a good thing. He didn't know how he became blue, but it did not matter. As long as the other animals treated him with awe, and left him food, he would make the most of it.

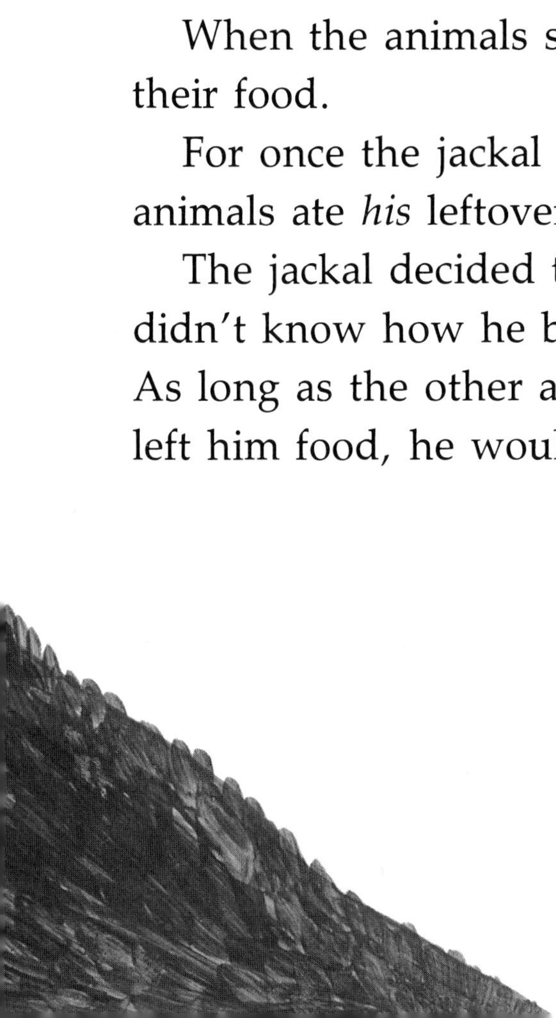

He told the other animals that they were right to keep their distance. He was special, indeed.

Had anyone seen a blue jackal before?

Of course not, he answered himself. There was no other animal like him.

He told the other animals that his color gave him extraordinary powers.

The animals were listening to him with rapt attention. He got carried away, and added, "Lord Krishna has made me blue in his image. He has also given me some of his special powers," the "blue" jackal told the spellbound assembly.

The gullible animals swallowed this boast. They started to treat the exotic blue jackal as someone unique, and would cater to his every wish and demand for food.

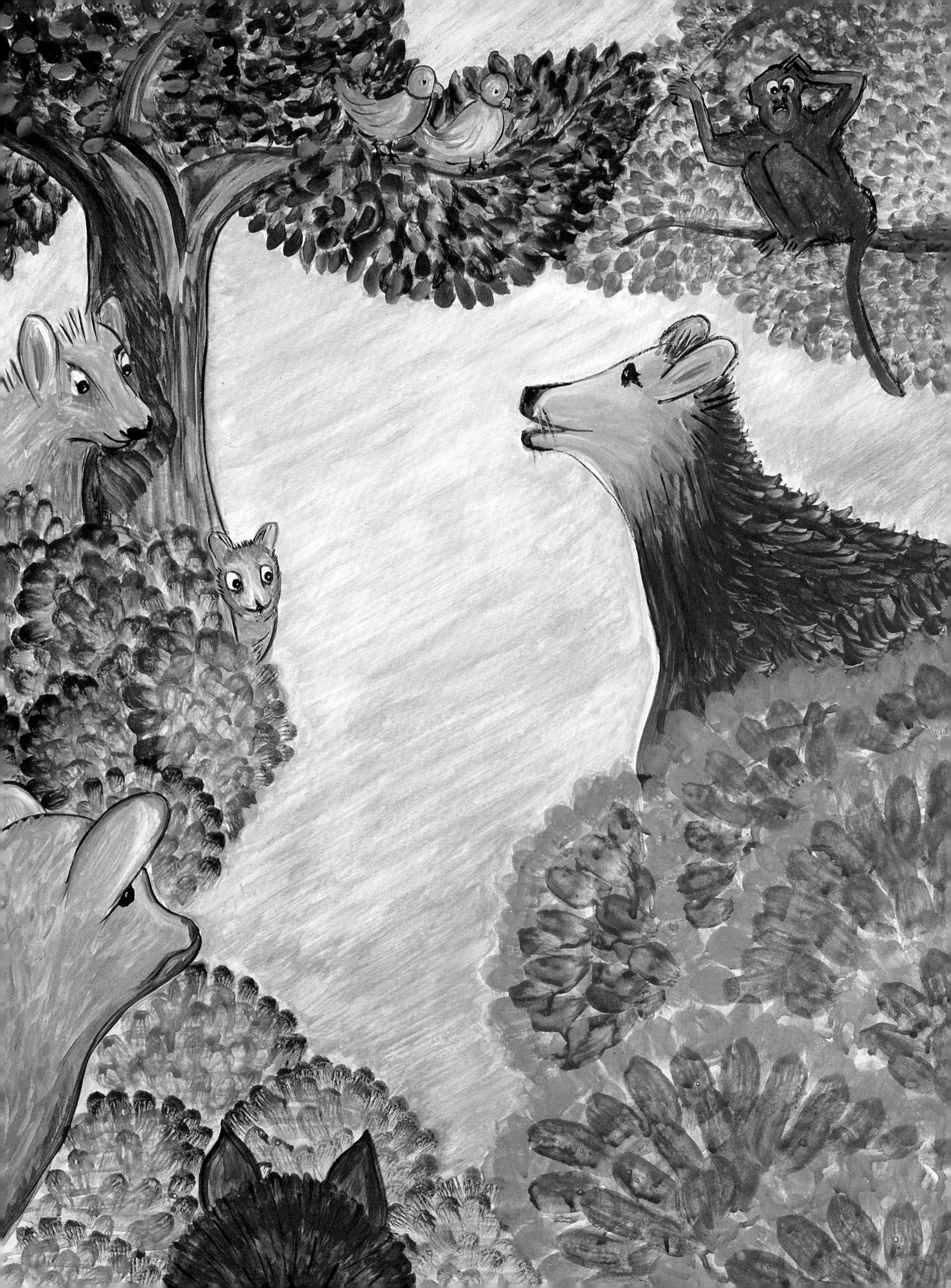

So the blue jackal lived royally. He had no more problems getting food, and for fear of Lord Krishna, none of the other animals dared to bother him.

This went on until the long awaited monsoon rains came.

Just when the animals felt that they could not stand the stifling heat anymore, the sky got dark with rain clouds.

Everyone looked up, hoping the monsoon rain would fall soon.

An expectant hush fell over the jungle.

The sky got darker still. There was a distant roar of thunder. Suddenly, the rain began to fall in great cool showers.

The heat was finally over! The water hole would fill up again. The land would become green and lush again.

The animals danced for joy!

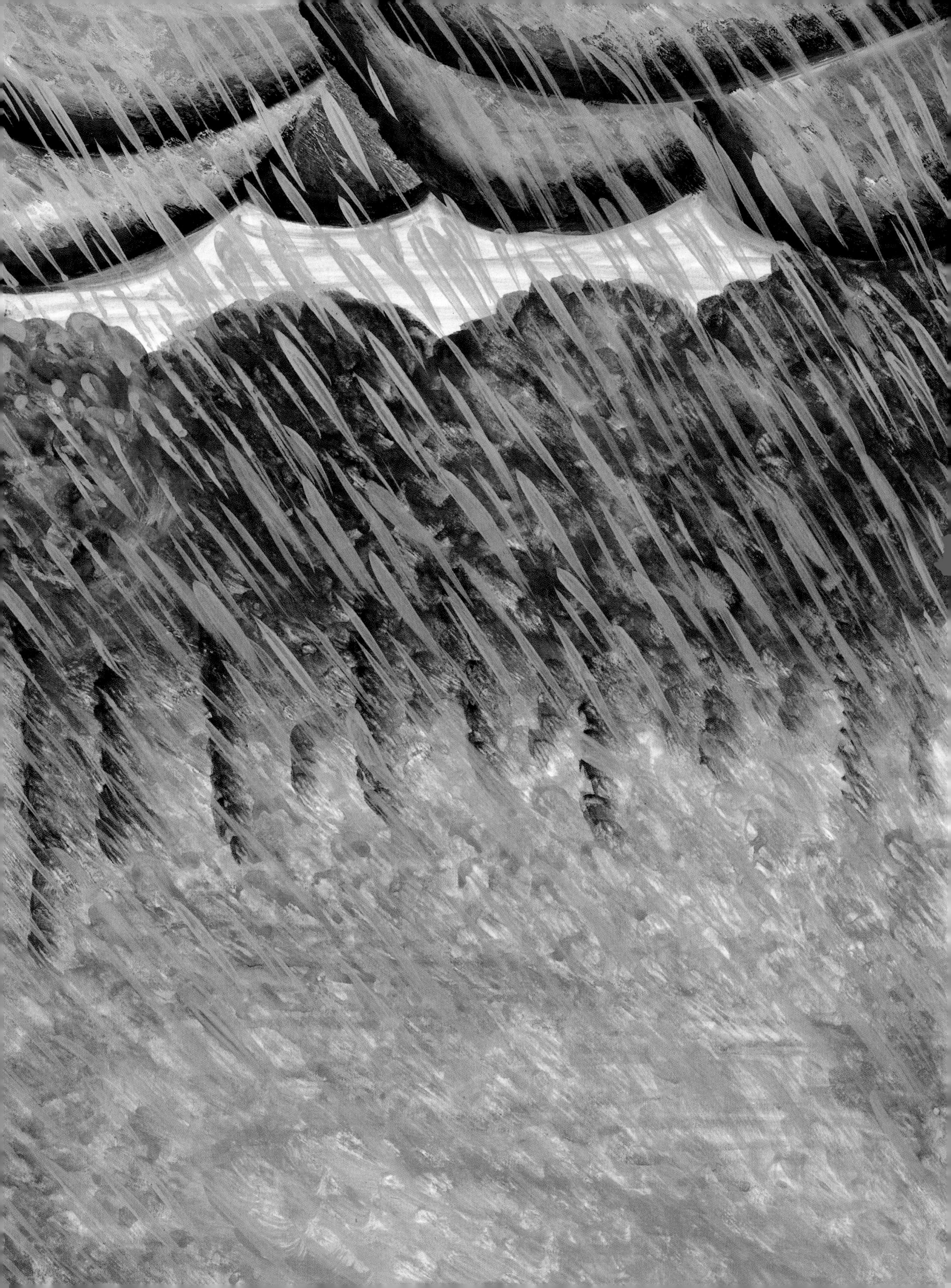

The blue jackal didn't join the ordinary animals in the dancing, but he too was happy.

Soon the jackal, too, got carried away enough to dance and jump with joy. After the heat of an Indian summer, splashing and playing in the falling rain was fun.

He was having such a good time that he did not notice some of the animals staring at him. They were whispering to each other and pointing at him.

"I thought Lord Krishna made you blue," said a monkey, yelling over the noise of the falling rain.

"He's a fake!" shouted a startled fox.

The jackal looked down, and saw that the rain showers and his dancing had washed off most of the blue (dye) from his fur. There was a tell-tale blue stain on the ground under him.

He got nervous.

The animals were now starting to look menacingly at him, and some of them were advancing towards him.

The jackal was really scared. The free ride was over. The animals were closing in on him!

Letting out a scared yowl of a jackal, he took off running.

Hearing that yowl, the animals stopped in their tracks. They had been tricked. He may have looked different, but there was no doubt that the "blue" jackal was an ordinary jackal, after all.

"He made us treat him as if he was special," mumbled a surprised fox.

"Lord Krishna's favorite!" laughed a hyena, pointing at the disappearing back of the 'blue' jackal.

"Just an ordinary jackal", hee-hawed a donkey.

"Tricked us all, tricked us all," mocked a laughing parrot.

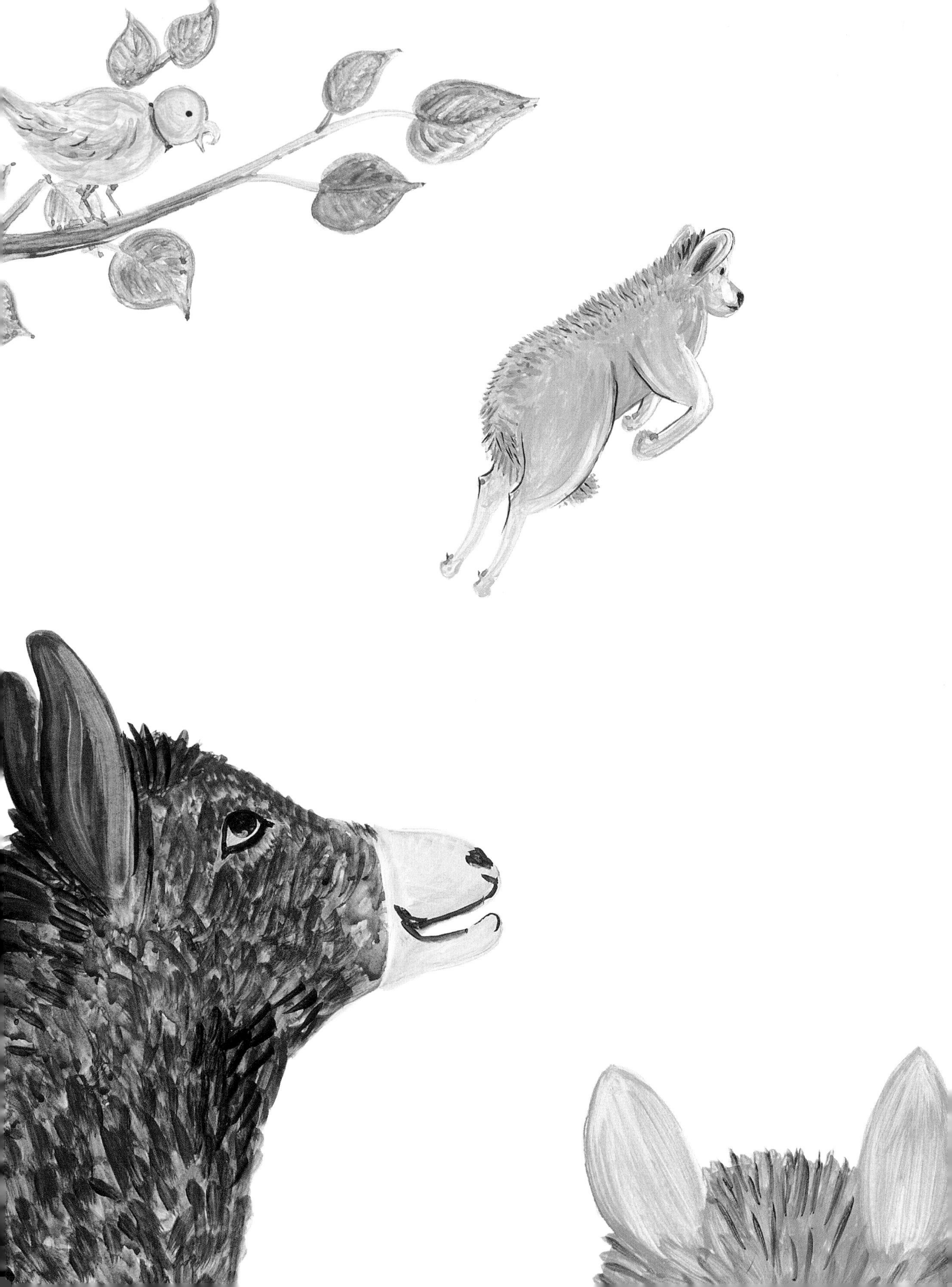

The animals felt too ashamed to admit that they had been tricked, so they left him alone. Instead of getting angry, they decided to treat the jackal's trick as a joke.

The jackal made sure that he lived at a respectful distance from the animals he had tricked.

From that day onward, whenever anyone put on airs, or expected to be treated better than others, the rest of the animals in the jungle would remind each other about the trick of the "blue" jackal.

Shanti
शांति

ABOUT PUNCHTUNTRA STORIES. . .

The Punchtuntra is a vast repertoire of children's stories in India. These are enjoyed by children of all ages, and fall under many categories – folktales/fables/children's tales/Indian stories/ancient literature.

The original was a collection of animal stories, in fable form. The animals had human characteristics which allowed them to live, think, feel and speak as humans.

For the Indian people, who still believe in the transmigration of the soul from human to animal and vice-versa, this human quality attributed to animals was not a hard feat of the imagination. The affinity of all living things is part of Indian beliefs.

The Punchtuntra is, in its original form, a main 'frame' story with many tales and fables nested within each other, sometimes three layers deep. It is written in a combination of Sanskrit prose and verse.

It has been attributed to a brahmin named Vishnu Sharman, although later versions of the same were attributed to Bidpai.

Vishnu Sharman, according to the traditional oral form of history in India, used these stories to educate three lazy sons of King Amar Shakti in the skills needed of Royal Princes. The king was in despair over his three spoilt sons. They thought that their lifestyle, assured by birth, meant that they needed no education. Since the traditional modes of education would take years (Sanskrit's grammar alone took 12 years!), Vishnu Sharman, a scholar-priest, hit upon the notion of instilling some skills and knowledge in the three potential heirs to the throne through simple anecdotal animal fables. The spoilt princes, who would not submit to formal education, were willing to try this method of effortless education.

At a later time in India's history, Bidpai used these same fables to extricate himself from a politically explosive situation with King Dabshalim.

Dabshalim was an Indian King in northwestern India who had defeated the Greek Governor left behind by Alexander 'the Great' who invaded India in 327-325 BCE. He commanded Bidpai to counsel him, but an honest answer would have meant severe punishment, or even death, for insolence towards the King. Bidpai had already enjoyed the hospitality of the King's royal dungeons and prison, so he had to be very careful how he answered the King's questions. The Punchtuntra stories, universally applicable, came to the rescue.

Bidpai chose the mask of animal stories to deal with the King. This method allowed for criticism and gentle comedy about human foibles and Royal mistakes without direct offence, without costing Bidpai his life or his integrity.

Fame of these remarkable stories spread along the trade routes to neighboring kingdoms of Asia.

The earliest known record of these in another land/language is in Persian in the sixth century. The King of Persia, it is said, wanted to be entertained by these remarkable Punchtuntra stories as well. He sent his physician to India, under the guise of searching for medicinal knowledge. The physician's real task was to find the wonderful repertoire of stories and fables referred to as Punchtuntra, and take these back to the King of Persia for his entertainment. The Royal Physician, having found these fables and stories, returned to Persia. These stories came to be known in Persian as Kalila wa Dimna.

From Persia these tales again travelled along the trade routes, being translated from Sanskrit into Persian to Arabic, to Hebrew, to Latin, to Spanish, to Italian, to German, and English, etc. Along the way each story was added to, modified, and adapted to suit local traditions.

Some scholars connect these tales to the African Aesop, whose tales became the basis for many western fables, from La Fontaine to Grimm's Tales, and even Chaucer.

As simple individual tales, these Punchtuntra stories are examples of classical literature from India which can still be enjoyed by children of all ages.

The story in this book is based on one of the Punchtuntra stories. India is a land of many cultures, settled over thousands of years by diverse races and people of varied complexions. Some people are as fair as Europeans, others as pigmented as Africans, with all the shades of brown in-between. The story of The Blue Jackal is told in India to instill the idea of a color-blind society, as opposed to superiority of one race based on skin color.

The use of humor, in a story supposedly about animals, has long been a successful method of getting a complex message across in simple understandable terms.

In a multi-ethnic world, this same story can be of use in making children think beyond superficial differences between diverse people, while encouraging the idea of equality among the global human family.

Copies of this book can also be purchased directly from the publisher.

VIDYA BOOKS
P.O. Box 7788
Berkeley, CA 94707-0788
Fax/Phone: (510) 527-9932